Henry and the Fox

Chris Wormell

Red Fox

This is Henry, and Henry is a coward.

Cockerels are usually proud and self-important.

They strut around farmyards bossing everybody else about and crowing boastfully.

But not this one.

Look at him – what a miserable-looking cockerel!

His crowing was awful – he sounded like a squeaky water pump. And whenever he tried bossing the hens about, they just ignored him.

Henry and the Fox

For Ned and Hector

HENRY AND THE FOX
A RED FOX BOOK 978 0 099 48383 0

First published in Great Britain by Jonathan Cape,
an imprint of Random House Children's Books

Jonathan Cape edition published 2006
Red Fox edition published 2007

1 3 5 7 9 10 8 6 4 2

Copyright © Chris Wormell, 2006

The right of Chris Wormell to be identified as the author and
illustrator of this work has been asserted in accordance
with the Copyright, Designs and Patents Act 1988.

All rights reserved.

Red Fox Books are published by Random House Children's Books,
61–63 Uxbridge Road, London W5 5SA

www.**kids**at**randomhouse**.co.uk

Addresses for companies within The Random House Group Limited
can be found at: www.randomhouse.co.uk/offices.htm

THE RANDOM HOUSE GROUP Limited Reg. No. 954009

A CIP catalogue record for this book is available from the British Library

Printed in Singapore

A cowardly cockerel is no use to anyone.

"He won't say 'boo' to a goose!" complained the hens. And it was true, he wouldn't. Nor would he say "tut-tut" to a turkey...

or "poo" to a piglet.

And as for mice . . .

Everyone thought poor Henry was hopeless. He had only one friend in the whole world: a bantam called Buffy. She was the smallest hen in the farmyard and was picked on and pecked by all the others, so she was miserable too.

One day Buffy and Henry were moping by themselves in the nettle bed, when Buffy, who was a clever little hen, suddenly cried:

"I have a plan!"

"A plan?" asked Henry.

"Yes, a brilliant plan! Wait here a moment."

Henry watched as Buffy ran across to where the farmer's wife had just hung out the washing.

She jumped up and caught hold of a long red sock, which she tugged and tugged and at last pulled free of its peg. Then she dragged it back to the nettle bed.

"There! What does that look like?" asked Buffy.

"Er . . . a rather damp red sock?" replied Henry.

Buffy sighed and shook her head. "Here, hold it open while I fill it."

Henry held up the sock and Buffy stuffed it with grass and leaves.

"There! Now what does it look like?"

"Er . . . a damp red sock filled with grass and leaves?" suggested Henry.

"Twit!" snapped Buffy, dragging the sock off to the middle of the nettle bed and leaving it there, half hidden.

"*Now* what do you see?" she demanded.

Henry thought for a long time.

"Er . . . a damp red sock filled with grass and leaves hidden in a nettle bed?" he said.

"Fool! It's a fox tail, isn't it?"

"Is it? Help!" Henry jumped at the word "fox".

"Yes, it's the bushy tail of a fox who's sleeping among the nettles; a fox that you, the brave cockerel, are going to chase out of there."

"Am I?" asked Henry, rather surprised. "But I'm not br — I'm . . . Oh, I *see*! . . .

"What a brilliant plan, Buffy!"

"I said it was, didn't I? Now, we just need one last thing."

"What's that?"

"The red woolly jumper hanging there on the washing line. Only I won't be able to pull it down; you'll have to."

They ran back over to the washing line and Henry tugged at the jumper until it came free, then dragged it back to the nettle bed.

"There!" said Buffy, arranging the red woolly jumper beside the stuffed sock in the middle of the nettles. "Now stand back over there and tell me what you see."

Henry had got the hang of it by now.

"I see a fox!" he replied. "A big bad fox, sleeping in the nettle bed!"

"Bravo!" cried Buffy. "Now, you wander off and presently I shall raise the alarm and then . . . well, you'll know what to do, won't you?"

"I will," said Henry.

It *was* a brilliant plan, wasn't it? And I am sure it would have worked perfectly. Only there was a problem. Actually there were *two* problems. The first was a large red hen called Rhoda.

Rhoda was strutting around the farmyard when she noticed the odd goings-on over at the washing line...

And very quietly she crept up and hid behind the wall next to the nettle bed . . .

It didn't take Rhoda long to realize what Buffy and Henry were up to.

"Ha! Silly fools!" she chuckled to herself. "We'll have some fun now," and she went off to tell the other hens what she had seen.

The other hens were scratching about in the corner of the paddock when little Buffy Bantam came running over, crying, "Help! Help! A fox! A fox!"

Rhoda gave them a big wink. "Oh, help!" she exclaimed. "Whatever shall we do? Who will save us from this terrible fox?"

At that moment, Henry appeared.

"Don't panic, ladies, don't panic!" he crowed. "I'll take care of this. Now, Buffy, where did you see this pesky fox?"

"In the nettle bed!" cried Buffy excitedly. "He's asleep in the nettle bed."

Henry marched off towards the nettle bed with Buffy and Rhoda and all the other chickens trailing along behind him. There was giggling and mutterings of "jumper" and "sock" among the hens at the back until Rhoda silenced them, saying with a sharp whisper, "Sshh! You'll spoil the fun!"

When they reached the edge of the nettles, Henry turned and said, "Now, ladies, you must all wait here. It's far too dangerous for you to go further. But don't worry, I'll soon sort out this fox."

If they stood on tiptoes, the chickens could see what certainly seemed to be a fox, curled up among the nettles.

"But Mr Henry, sir, aren't you afraid?" gasped Buffy.

"Well, one has to be brave," replied Henry in a casual manner.

They all watched as Henry carefully picked his way among the stems until he was right in the middle of the nettle bed. Then, in a flurry of feathers, he leaped onto the red woolly jumper.

And now we come to the second problem.

The hot sun had quickly dried out the woolly jumper and turned it into a soft, warm, inviting bed. Such a soft, warm, inviting bed that, while Buffy was off raising the alarm, someone had come along, and curled up, and fallen asleep on it . . .

And that someone was a fox!

A fox who was now having a most delicious dream; a dream of lovely, fat, plucked chickens; lots and lots of lovely, fat, plucked chickens.

He was just getting to the good part – the gobbling-up part –
when the dream suddenly turned into a nightmare and all those
lovely, fat, plucked chickens got up and jumped on top of him!

And imagine his horror on finding that his nightmare had come true! *Never* had he been attacked by a chicken before.

Poor Henry got a terrible shock when the red woolly jumper turned into a *real* fox. He opened his beak to scream, only that's not what came out. What came out was a glorious
        "COCK-A-DOODLE-DOO!"
right in the fox's face.

The fox ran for his life.

And Henry *would* have run for his life, but his legs were too wobbly.
Buffy and Rhoda and all the other hens were struck dumb
with amazement until Buffy cried at the top of her voice, "Bravo!"

After that the chickens never called Henry a coward again.
And indeed he really seemed to have changed. He'd gained a
certain confidence and would even venture a "boo" at the geese,
or a "tut-tut" to the turkey.

And woe betide any piglets that gave him trouble!

Though he was never bossy, he made sure no one ever picked on little Buffy Bantam again. Best of all, he'd learned how to crow, and every morning he repeated that glorious

"COCK-A-DOODLE-DOO!"

But he was still afraid of mice . . .